Septen

For Cas + Bob,

♡

Donald J. Malcohn

MW00712704

My Own True Story

TIRAMISÙ

as told to **Donald James Malcolm**

sweetgrassbooks
an imprint of Farcountry Press

DEDICATION

Dedicated to my dear and lovely wife, Laura, who always encouraged me with her wisdom, gentleness, and love. She loved Tiramisu and believed in his story as a message of the healing power of love. Many thanks, my dear Laura.

ISBN: 978-1-59152-296-6

© 2021 by Donald James Malcom

All rights reserved. This book may not be reproduced in whole or in part by any means (with the exception of short quotes for the purpose of review) without the permission of the publisher. For more information, call 435-313-4997.

For more information or to order extra copies of this book call Farcountry Press toll free at (800) 821-3874.

sweetgrassbooks
an imprint of Farcountry Press

Produced by Sweetgrass Books; PO Box 5630, Helena, MT 59604; (800) 821-3874; www.sweetgrassbooks.com.

Printed in Canada.
Produced in the United States of America.

24 23 22 21   1 2 3 4

PROLOGUE

The story of Tiramisù began with a phone call from our dear friend, Giovanna. It was not the normal chatting of, "How are you doing?" and, "Good to hear your voice," but rather a very serious, and somewhat desperate request. "Donald and Laura, could you please, please consider adopting a kitten?"

Giovanna had found an abandoned baby kitten whimpering in the countryside ditch just outside of her property gate. The kitten was in a perilous state and Giovanna had no possibility of taking it in considering the fact that her dog was aggressive toward cats that were not of the family. The reality on our side was that we had already rescued around a dozen orphaned kittens, so the immediate answer to this urgent request was basically, "No, I don't think we can consider it."

All of the back and forth *no* and *yes* conversation with Giovanna finally came to a standstill.

However, in this standstill, my wife Laura and I both felt that this was not something we could easily brush off. It was a decision that we felt needed to be reflected upon and prayed about. For us, it was not a matter of, "Well, it is only a cat." Instead, we were dealing with a life in peril: yes, of a kitten, but to us it was a precious little creature crying out to be saved. The easy road would have been to ignore it or pretend it was nothing of great importance, convincing ourselves that we were not the answer to this problem.

It's like when we think or say, "Do I need another crisis in my life? Can't I have a little peace and quiet and not be disturbed by all of these cries and pleas?" Too often we reply, "This is not my responsibility."

After pondering, it did not take us long to call back and say, "Giovanna, we were very hesitant about taking another kitten, but after reflecting we feel good about it so bring him over."

Yes, this was "just a kitten" but this kitten to whom we said "Yes" turned out to be like an unexpected special package, a gift with a bow!

As so often happens in life, that which seems *scomodo* (inconvenient, uncomfortable, or troublesome) turns out to be a blessing, which, in this case brought lots of joy and patience and a good dose of laughs!

There was no doubt about it, Tiramisù was a special gift. He never took a break from generously pouring out his affection and love, and of course we showered on him the same. This was a lesson of what a blessing it means to give with no strings attached. Love prevailed in spite of the many moments of having to say, "Tiramisù, what are you up to now? You are a little rascal!" Yet, he was a most lovable scamp. After being scolded, he would beg—and even insist—that I pick him up and cuddle him in my arms. He had it figured out that we were very generous and forgiving and that all of his provocative antics usually ended up with us smiling and laughing. To Tiramisù, there was never too much love and affection, and he knew exactly how to get it. Yes, Tiramisù was quite a cat!!!

— *Donald J. Malcolm*

"Lord, you know the hopes of the helpless. Surely you will hear their cries and comfort them. You will bring justice to the orphans and the oppressed . . ."

Psalm 10:17,18a *The Holy Bible*—New Living Translation

❧ ❧ ❧

Facing page: Map of where Tiramisù lived in Italy.

Reggello: *Where Tiramisù was born in the Valdarno area of Tuscany.*

L'Uccellare: *Tiramisù's first home in the Chianti area of Tuscany near Florence.*

Ospedaletti: *Tiramisù's second home at Villa Nazareth in Liguria.*

Sanremo (San Remo): *Tiramisù's final home at Villa Gioiello in the city of Flowers and Music in Liguria.*

MISE-EN-SCÈNE

For Giovanna and the kitten to reach our home, L'Uccelare, they traveled down from her house in the foothills of the Tuscan Apennine mountains. After reaching the Arno river south of Florence, they proceeded up through the Chianti Classico hills which were covered with olive trees, vineyards, and the majestic cypresses; the quintessential image of Tuscany! The drive to reach our home could not be more beautiful. The Florentine hills are softly pastoral, bathed in the history of the Etruscans, the Romans, and that of the genius-filled Italian Renaissance, which touches one's soul and spirit to this day.

As they journeyed to our home, we waited, with great anticipation, to meet this new addition to our cat family. We had no idea how his life and ours would unfold into a marvelous and enriching chapter of unconditional love.

> *"Feed the hungry, and help those in trouble. Then your light will shine out from the darkness, and the darkness around you will be as bright as noon."*

Isaiah 58:10 *The Holy Bible*—New Living Translation

With This The Curtains Open!

What follows is the story and saga told through the voice and words of the wonderful Tiramisù! Let your imagination soar as Tiramisù shares his tale as only he can tell it, both funny and sobering. This is a true story—not a fable—of a life lived to its fullest with its ups and downs, blessings and troubles. 🐾

TIRAMISÙ

MY OWN TRUE STORY

Here I was, small, hungry, and afraid, crouched down in the grass hoping that something—or someone—would save me from being abandoned and most probably to die of hunger. All I could do was hope since I didn't know if the young lady would come back to give me something to eat or not. Every once in a while I would let out a whimper not knowing if it was even heard. Everything seemed so terribly hopeless.

But at the moment of my deepest despair, I heard the gate open and she softly called out to me. "Ciao, it's Giovanna . . . don't be scared . . . " When she saw me, she slowly lowered her hand down into the grass. In it she held a small dish of food. After I had a few bites, she quickly picked me up and took me directly to her car, where she placed me into a cat carrier. Obviously, I was quite afraid, but she was very gentle and continued to tell me that everything was going to be okay.

I did not really understand her Italian, but I could tell she was trying to keep me calm. Every so often she would softly reassure me, "Don't you worry, it's going to be okay." Even though I started to understand that "okay" meant don't worry or be afraid, I was still crouched down in fear in the cat carrier as we took off in her car. It was all very scary. The last time I was in a car I was tossed out into a roadside ditch with a rough, "Who needs another cat?"

As we sped down through the valleys and over the hills, she quietly sang and a sense of calm settled over me in the cage. I think it was her soft, lovely voice that soothed me; however, I had no idea what was going on nor did I know that we were heading toward my new home. I was very shaken, confused, and felt weak. "How long will I be in this cage?" I wondered. I had been assured by Giovanna that I was on my way to a good home, but how could I know that this would be true? As I said, the last time I was in a car, I was tossed out into a roadside ditch!

After some time and a very wild ride filled with curves and rough roads, we finally came to a halt. I had no idea where we were since I couldn't see a thing from the car. Giovanna got out and warmly exchanged greetings and kisses with her two friends who were waiting for her.

Giovanna seemed very relieved and happily declared, "Well, here is your new baby kitten!"

I got the picture that this was to be my final destination as she picked up the cat carrier and placed it down inside the courtyard. Of course, I am the surprise still in the cage!

Finally, the cage latch was opened and I slowly and cautiously stepped out. I felt very tense. It was great to be out of the cage and set free, but I was quite terrified! I took a deep breath and a few tentative steps. Gazing around, I realized I was surrounded by a beautiful garden and standing in front of a huge ancient stone house.

Our home—L'Uccellare.

Everything was bright and beautiful, but still scary! At that moment, the two very friendly people who were talking with Giovanna turned and spoke directly to me. I was introduced to them as Signor Donald and Signora Laura. I did not run away and panic as one may have expected.

They bent down and began to pet me with a soft and loving touch.

"Oh, look how tiny he is. He is probably no more than five or six weeks old."

"Don't you worry, we will take good care of you. You are very cute and sweet."

"He is all ears!"

Their voices were very warm and friendly, nothing like the ones I had heard the day I was abandoned on the roadside. Donald picked me up and held me very close and then he gently passed me into the arms of Laura. I had never experienced affection like this before and my fears quickly vanished. I felt totally safe and did not want to be put down. Considering all that I had been through, I could have just stayed put in those arms.

As they chatted, they continued to pet me and assure me that all would turn out for the best. They placed a small dish of milk and some cat food on the ground and put me down. I was not familiar with milk in a bowl, but Donald knew how to solve that problem. He just pushed my face gently into the milk. I got the picture as soon as I licked it off. No more instruction was needed! The cat food and milk like this was something I had never tasted. I believe he said that it was salmon pâté with spinach . . . very delicious! Donald encouraged me to eat and after the first bite, I knew that this was food of a totally different category. I loved it! From that day forward, I never had anything but the best gourmet delectable choices.

When I finished eating and looked up from my dish, I saw that I was surrounded by a menagerie of cats staring at me. I hadn't been paying too much attention, but upon my arrival I had obviously become the center of focus. I was in such a state of shock after all that had taken place in my life in these last few days that everything seemed surreal. I felt lucky just to be alive.

I could hear these cats were quietly asking each other, "Who is this? I wonder if he is going to be staying?"

"He was just dropped off by the young lady in the car, so I would say he is here to stay."

"He is certainly not European."

"Times are changing. You never know what's going to turn up."

"He is quite exotic looking. He has those blue eyes like a Siamese which we've seen more of in the last few years."

"Yes, he looks a lot like a—but no—he is certainly not a 'Rag Doll.' Those really are all the rage nowadays!"

"We have no idea if he speaks Catitalian, but I'm sure he will pick it up quickly."

Despite of all the surmising and supposing and speculating, they seemed quite friendly. No bad vibes. Not one of them came forward and pushed their face into my cat food or gave me a swat. Actually, it was a very warm welcome.

Donald and Laura looking down, referred to me as "the kitten" since I did not have yet a real name of my own. They said they wanted to introduce me to the lineup of family cats, one by one. It didn't take me long to remember their names and learn something of the story of their lives. They, like me, were all orphans lovingly brought into this family's home. In one way or another, all of us had gone through trauma and life-threatening experiences.

In the days following my arrival, I really felt like a transformed kitten. Instead of threatening voices, there were lots of gentle and kind words and "pick me up" hugs. This turned me around and helped me forget the horrible things that happened to me before coming here.

Now I want to introduce you to my new cat friends because they will become a big part of my life story.

The littlest kitten, Baby Calico Skies, was fairly new to the bunch. I mention her first because upon my arrival she came up and gave me a cat kiss. She was found close to midnight one evening on the dusty dirt road that descended over the hills down to this house. The fact that Donald and Laura even saw her in the car's headlights as she crawled out of the thick brush was a miracle. With one hand, Donald swept her up (she was no bigger than his palm) and put her into Laura's lap and she, tiny little thing, fell right to sleep. Well, Baby totally loved me, and did not hesitate to start licking my face and ears. I think she saw that I needed a little cleaning up!

All the other cats that were sitting and looking at me when I arrived were, as I said, also orphans and castaways. The first one adopted was Gioia who was found crying beside a dumpster in the countryside. Laura thought it was a bird chirping until she saw this kitten no bigger than a sparrow. She was so small that at first, she had to be fed with a doll's tiny baby bottle. In time, Gioia really became the queen. She was quick to remind all of us that she was the first cat to be the object of Donald and Laura's mercy and compassion.

Gioia

There were two other kittens, a brother and sister named Salvatore and Santolina. Their mother, Bellina, and her brother, Belloccio, who had been abandoned and left behind to fend for themselves by the previous owners of the L'Uccellare villa, were also present. Santolina and Salvatore would turn out to be my great friends as we were the same age. Santolina was named such because of her delight in jumping up and down on a very perfumed herbal plant called Santolina. Donald, who dearly loved her, would have to scold her for her persistent jumping and flattening of the Santolina plants under the olive tree. She would do this just about every day! Later, she had the misfortune of getting a serious virus in one of her eyes which the vet was not able to save. Despite this tragedy, she was not set back, and as before Santolina continued joyfully jumping and dancing around the courtyard. I, being the hunter, yet tender hearted, would always bring back my catch to the house and drop it at her feet.

Sometime after I arrived, a beautiful young tabby appeared out of the blue. Our "parents", Donald and Laura, were gone on a long trip and the English house sitters noticed him as he sauntered up to the large wrought iron gate. "It was as if he invited himself for tea one day and decided to stay," the English man said. He was totally relaxed, as if he had always lived there and had no intention of leaving. Of course, we knew

that Donald and Laura would adopt him upon their return, which they did. They named him Benjamin since he was, at that time, the last one to be part of our cat tribe. I was told this name came from a story in the Bible and Benjamin was the youngest of Jacob's twelve sons. He was an extremely lovable cat with a silky, cashmere-like coat. But unlike me, he did not like to be held and carried around. Benjamin had a habit of

making sure he was always getting the best of the food that was served at mealtimes. He would jump from plate to plate, not being able to stand the idea that another cat just *might* get something more tasty than what was on his plate. Really, it was rather rude of him, but we tolerated it without discussion.

It is true, we were fed gourmet style with lots of variety. Donald would always come home loaded down with heavy bags of cat food. We were curious about what new recipe the pet store would dream up. There was no doubt it would be a special shrimp or sardine delight or perhaps chicken with an oriental flair. I think I heard Donald say that only food lovers like the Italians could come up with these choices. We certainly did not complain. Were our meals better than what most people eat? Yes, I think I can say that is true. So, even if Benjamin was a little pushy for my liking, this did not affect our friendship and we always stayed close.

This sums up my introduction to the cat family up to this point!

Now, I want to take you back to the first days following my arrival at the L'Uccellare home. The day after my landing, I literally collapsed and nearly died. No one knew this, but when Giovanna brought me to L'Uccellare I was sick, yes, very sick. The trauma of being wickedly abandoned left me in a very fragile and pathetic state. I didn't look so bad on the outside—no cuts or bruises—I was just a little skinny. But on this particular morning, I fell flat on the stone courtyard and was not able to stand up. My new parents panicked and couldn't believe what was happening!

They quickly rushed me to the nearest vet, Dr. Enrico. There, I was examined, and given a shot and an intravenous treatment, all with the hope that it would revive me. Everyone was very worried seeing that my situation was so precarious and certainly did not look encouraging. The medical tests showed that I had some kind of virus which was no doubt made worse by all the trauma I had been through. We returned home, and all the while Laura and Donald were hoping and praying for the best. In the days that followed I was showered with loads of care and so much love. I pulled through and all seemed fine even though I was still very frail.

With all of the confusion in those first days, I ended up still being just "the kitten". Donald kept saying to Laura that they had to come up with a good name for me. He said, "We can't just keep calling him the kitten."

One afternoon when I was snuggling with them on the bench in the courtyard, they held me up and asked, "What should we name you? It can't be something banal."

Of course, I couldn't make any suggestions in a language they would understand so I just waited and waited for my new name. Donald and Laura went back and forth with various names: Cappuccino, Caffe Latte, Chocolate Delight, and Cream Puff . . . all because of the coloration of my fur. Can you imagine having to go around living with one of those names? Thank goodness they dropped those!

Potted flowers are pretty, but potted cats are hilarious!

Great view—but when are they going to get the pool going?

Donald paused, then declared, "No, these will never do. You are too special to have a silly name like that! No, you will be Tiramisù!"

Tiramisù! Now *that* was a name I really liked! In Italian it means "lift me up" or that which gets you going after an illness or a trauma.

You can hardly imagine how perfectly that name fits me! I have dark chocolate-colored ears, what looks like a bandit's mask on my face, a mocha coffee-colored fur coat, and a mascarpone cream-colored tummy and paws. The point is this: chocolate, espresso, and mascarpone make up the delicious Tiramisù dessert! To top it all off, I have the most beautiful blue eyes you could imagine. Most everyone says that I am unusual; not strange, but unusual and beautiful. This is partly because I am a Snowshoe cat, very rare and yes, different from the common European cat.

Upon seeing me people often exclaim, "Tiramisù, come sei bello!" which means *you are very handsome* in Italian.

I take that compliment quite seriously, pleased that they are noticing how handsome and exotic I am. Yes, interesting, I'd been a nobody and not wanted, then Donald and Laura adopted me, their "baby", and gave me my own special name, **TIRAMISÙ!**

I was never considered a house cat and I was not afraid of ending up in a cat fight. I have claws that are super long and sharp and we cats know how to use our claws and keep them sharp by scraping up and down on a tree trunk; however, to be honest, sometimes I would lose a fight. One day, I returned home barely able to crawl into the courtyard. With no strength and no desire to eat I caved in and plopped flat out on the stones. All I could do was lay there motionless, almost without life. Donald and Laura were terribly shaken and rushed me off to the vet again. (A few months earlier, Salvatore, my new cat buddy, had similar symptoms and the condition was quite grave.) Into the cat carrier I went. Up and down and over the hills and through the winding rough roads we drove to the clinic. All the while, Donald and Laura praying that I could be saved from death. They prayed because they knew that God loved and cared for even a little cat like me!

Dr. Enrico pulled my weak body out of the carrier and placed me onto a cold, shiny steel table. He looked me over and then, lifting my painfully swollen paw said, "Oh yes, here it is. He has been bitten and traumatized. We need to check him for AIDS!" With a needle, he drew some blood and then we waited for the verdict. Soberly, Dr. Enrico said, "Look at these dots on the blood slide. This indicates that he has feline AIDS. There is no cure and even a simple cold or trauma can kill him. You must understand, he is fragile and has no defenses. He may not have a very long life: no one knows."

There was silence. Donald and Laura almost wept.

I got an injection. In the following days I was showered with SO much love and cuddling. Being HIV positive, you never can be cured . . . you carry it always.

But, surprise! Very soon, only a day or so, I felt totally well with all of my energy, and I went right back to hunting and exploring.

Every so often I get into trouble, a terrible scare with a hunter's dog or a bad fight with a big stray tomcat. Whenever this happens, there I am sick and motionless, barely able to walk. Donald and Laura know that there is one way to help pull me through. I say "help" because it doesn't guarantee anything. They give me a little antibiotic which I hate to take and basically refuse. But no medicine, no help!

So, Donald got a chocolate-flavored antibiotic paste to smear on my paw. Now what cat likes having a paste smeared on their paw? We have a mania for being clean. So, what do we do? We lick it off. That's the trick. We lick it off, swallow it, and guess what? It tastes like chocolate. Pretty clever. But sometimes the pharmacy doesn't have the chocolate paste, so we have to go back to those bitter green pills. *Schifo!* In Italian, that means disgustingly nasty! However, my Donald came up with a new idea: crush the pill and mix it with anchovy paste. Here we go again—paste on the paw, lick the paw—and who can taste a pill when it's covered with delicious anchovy paste?

But the REAL CURE for my desperate state is to be smothered by those cuddles and loving words, not by anchovy paste.

Yes, you may be thinking, "You have already told us how love and cuddles helps you revive." Yes, and I will continue to sing its praises because sometimes after being totally flat out—and I mean not even being able to walk—I feel like I am "healed" and feel quite normal simply because Donald picks me up to cuddle me in his arms. This is the therapy and power of LOVE. My health concerns are not, unfortunately, those that get healed once and for all. They are repeated very often and so, too, is the repeated power of love and kindness, year after year, bringing me healing and hope.

So you are probably thinking, this Tiramisù sounds like he is total delight. Well, it isn't *exactly* that way. Scamp and "A Real Pain in the Neck" could also be names for me. We Snowshoe cats like to talk, so I invented all types of sounds to get Donald's attention: a whining, begging cry when I want to be let inside, a simple sweet meow which usually means, "Pick me up, please!" and a moaning wail as if to say, "I'll commit suicide if you don't rescue me from this second-floor window railing this instant!" I even got so I could cry out "Dooonnnald" which would scare the wits out of him and Laura both.

I have big ears and an even bigger intelligence, or so say Donald and Laura. For example, if I am outside, I can figure out exactly what Donald and Laura are doing most of the time, even where they are in the house,

Okay, okay, Tiramisu, we will rescue you before you fall off into space.

and the house is enormous! If they sit down to a meal when I am outside, within 60 seconds, I scoot around the house and sit in full sight with my nose pressed on the floor-to-ceiling glass sliding door, yowling as they are saying grace over their meal. "Buon Appetito, Donald and Laura!" What an interruption that is!

Am I hungry? No, not really; I just like attention. I wait for Donald—who is quite irritated and knows that I will never shut up—to open the sliding glass door. I jump through and do a fast run across the house and quickly exit out the front door opened by Donald with his scolding "Ciao, Ciao" which is another way of saying, "See you later . . . much later!!! And if you can believe it, often I do a quick house turnaround and repeat the same annoying routine!

Sometimes, I get to sleep on their bed. But being who I am, I like a little action at 3:00 am. When laying between Donald and Laura I reach over and put my paw on Donald's cheek, or I give the pull chain of the bedside lamp a nice swat. Ting, ting!! Do they wake up? Of course they do! When Laura started threatening to "put that cat out immediately!" I learned a new trick. If she stirs because of my middle-of-the-night antics I PLAY DEAD! I act as if I am totally asleep and don't make a move until I am sure that Laura has gone back to sleep. I then continue annoying my Donald with that lamp-chain-swat. Ting, ting!! Do you think he can sleep? Of course not!

Oh, I have other special traits. Early in the morning or at night, when Donald comes outside into the courtyard to greet us or just to check that all things are in order, I often sneak up behind him and reach my front paws way up and try to pull his pajama bottoms off. He gets quite irritated with me and doesn't think it such a cute joke, especially when my sharp claws go through the flannel pajamas and into his hide!

Another time—but not the only time!—I grew bored in the middle of the night so I decided to give Donald and Laura a visit and maybe cuddle in with them. This was no small feat. To reach the tall second floor windows that open into their bedroom, I had to climb up a terrace pergola, onto a tiled roof, and then leap four to five feet up from there onto a metal railing against the large windows of their bedroom. Sound a little complicated? Well, it was no problem for me.

Once on the roof, I gave out a call before leaping up onto the narrow railing just to let them know I was coming. Amazing, but as I have already mentioned, I somehow learned to say Donald's name in my cat talk, so I let out a loud "Dooonnnald!" Of course, Donald, who has good hearing, heard someone calling out his name in the middle of the night. Such a thing would be rather unusual seeing that we lived off the beaten path in Chianti. Startled, he woke up Laura and I heard him say, "Listen, someone is calling out my name!"

Guess who is coming to pay us a visit?

Laura sounded frightened and replied, "Yes . . . they are calling your name, but who could that be at 3 o'clock in the morning?!"

They listened and sure enough heard another, "Dooonnnald! Dooonnnald!" This became a little scary!

Donald got up in disbelief and said, "Laura, I can't believe it, but I think it is Tiramisù. Yes, here he is out on the railing wanting in. Oh, my goodness, now what? We have him calling out my name in the middle of the night!"

Of course, I thought it was too cute and they let me in. I curled up in the bed, waiting until Laura was asleep again, and then started patting Donald on the cheek. How can one sleep when someone—me, the cat— pats you on the cheek?

One of my favorite things? Lizard hunts—any size or color will do. Mice are also fun, but lizards are the most exciting. I don't kill or eat them, but a little torture, yes, until Donald sets them free. I don't give up easily! One time I went way down the hill across the plowed field to explore and guess what I found in the grass? A HUGE BRIGHT GREEN LIZARD about 14 inches long. I caught him and carried him like a hot dog in my mouth, tail sticking out on one side and his head out the other, without hurting him or getting bitten. I treaded all the way back up the hill over the plowed furrows to show Donald. *Come sono bravo!* How great and brave I am! Despite my resistance, Donald insisted that I set him free, which I finally did.

I was not the only cat going off on adventures. Baby Calico Skies had this frequent mysterious routine of taking off in the morning—all by herself—and disappearing down our country road. This road had only a couple of houses perched on a steep hillside before it dead-ended at a stream. I did this walk a few times, and it seemed a little dangerous and crazy for a cat never knowing what you might run into. After an hour or two, Baby would be seen making her way back up the road to our house.

Tiramisu, Salvatore, and Jack

Always upon arrival she smelled of an exotic rose perfume! All us cats could smell it—and Donald and Laura as well—because they would comment on it and ask her what she'd been up to. Of course, she never did give us an answer. We concluded that there was probably a very perfumed lady down that road that cuddled her each day. Who knows? We never did resolve that mystery.

There were a number of times when we were left at L'Uccellare because Donald and Laura were absent for commitments in Florence or for trips abroad. When they were gone, they always had someone come by daily and check that we were alright and feed us. Because of security issues, someone would also check around the house for problems. Once, there was a broken water pipe which flooded the ancient wine cellar. Fortunately, Donald and Laura returned that very day and saved us from a flooded house! On two occasions, however, when no one but us cats were home, we had break-ins by gypsies. We knew that these were evil characters up to no good coming in the darkness of the night. But what were we to do? Ambush them and claw their backs and faces before they escaped into the dark? Maybe we could have tried, but we just stayed hidden out of sight. After these robberies, wrought-iron grills went up on the windows and doors, and lots of outdoor automatic lighting. There was another break-in attempt, but Donald got the military police with a helicopter to go after them.

Please understand that we lived in a rather remote area of Chianti, surrounded by hills covered with vineyards and olive groves, with deep valleys of thick forests of cypresses and oaks. One would only consider entering these scary forests with much caution because they were often filled with herds of wild boar. Very aggressive critters! At most, only two to three cars would pass by our home in a day's time and the road ended in a deep valley with a river no car could cross. The cats, including me, never ventured down into that territory.

Seeing that we were isolated didn't mean that there was no life around. Most of the "life" came out after sundown. Summer and fall nights we would hear a loud rush in the field coming toward the house with aggressive grunting and squealing. Usually, it was about 30 wild boar: cute piglets, nervous mamas, and enormous boars. They headed straight for the orchards of apricots, plums, and walnuts, devouring the fallen fruit and loudly crunching the pits. Really there was only one who was The King and he was as big as a Fiat Cinquecento. When startled by Donald and his flashlight, The King would give a booming snort and all the boars, big and small, would turn in a rush and head to the forest as fast as they could. You would never want to run into them with those huge sharp tusks!

Us cats just watched the whole scene from up in a tree or on top of a roof. In our area there were savage polecats called *faina* which would climb up on the tiled roof looking for bird's nests to get the eggs . . . or even the birds. However, their specialty was killing people's chickens and ducks. Thankfully, Donald and Laura had none of these for them to hunt. They never actually tried to touch us, but they were scary varmints!

We had the all-too-often night visit of the *istrici*, a very, very large and fast-moving porcupine with 12- to 15-inch sharp quills. Donald had, with much work, just planted two 100-foot-long rows of iris rhizomes in a new garden field with the hope of enjoying their beauty come spring. Surprise! A couple of days after the planting, he discovered that ALL of the rhizomes had been dug up and devoured by the *istrici*. As Donald said, "Nothing like having your beautiful balloon pop!"

One unsettling mystery was when a car would come slowly down our road late at night. All of us cats wondered, "Who can that be at this hour?" The car would pass by our home and then park out of sight at the lower end of our vineyard. We'd hear the sound of voices and the opening and shutting of car doors. Donald would take a large flashlight and shine it down to where they were, so they got the picture that they were being monitored, even if not seen. It made us all a little uneasy. Donald concluded that it was no doubt a drug exchange with someone from down by the river. With his continual flashing of the light these appointments never lasted very long. One thing to remember is we cats slept outside in the cat house in the protected courtyard and that is why we got to be part of all this "night life."

On the tamer side, we frequently had deer come through the gardens and orchards. There was the small *daino*, the *cervo* (mule deer), and the rare and magnificent stags. One day, out of the window of Donald's study where I often spent time with him, we saw in the upper garden two beautiful full antler-adorned stags. Neither of us could believe our eyes. But there was a downside to their regal presence: they loved to munch the rose buds and sharpen their antlers on the almond trees.

The worst enemy for us cats, and for Donald and Laura, were the hunters and their dogs. They had no respect for private property and would come right up to the house. The dogs went crazy trying to catch us cats. If caught we would surely be killed, so at the first sign of the hunters' presence we would flee and hide where the dogs could not reach us. Donald asked the hunters to stay away from the house and control their dogs, all to no avail! Their aggressive, disrespectful behavior was deeply engrained. Private property meant nothing to them and they let you know it, even arrogantly firing a rain of lead pellets over Donald's head because he asked them to park their vehicle along the road and not in our muddy field. We survived the season of pheasant and wild boar hunting thanks to divine protection. As you can see, we were not lazy and pampered cats, sleeping all day on a sofa with soft classical music playing.

As I said earlier, I am somewhat of a super tomcat. Even though I was castrated at the proper age, I didn't act like it, and perhaps didn't even believe it. The interesting thing is that a few years after I arrived at L'Uccellare, a bunch of kittens appeared up the road from where I lived.

One of them looked very much like you-know-who: Tiramisù! You must understand that Snowshoe cats like me are very rare and have a very distinctive coat coloring and blue eyes; therefore, you didn't see one around every corner!

Well, my parents, Donald and Laura, were asking themselves, "How did this happen? Even Dr. Enrico said, "Sometimes funny things happen, but I promise you I DID do the operation!" This kitten up the road disappeared and only some time later did Donald see him alone in the dense forest. It seemed as if he had no home and had been abandoned. Donald so much wanted to save him, but by this time he was quite wild and difficult to approach.

Then one cold rainy night he appeared, wet and bloody, on the court-yard stone wall. It looked as if he had been attacked by some wild animal. All of us cats watched with fixed eyes as he stared back at us. It seemed that he wanted to join us. Had he caught a scent in the air or had an intuition that this was the place where he would receive help? By chance, Donald sensed that something was stirring as he stepped out into the dark, rainy courtyard. Looking around he saw this drenched cat standing on the stone wall. Donald was stunned to see him right before his eyes after all his hopes and prayers to save him from who knows what. He had basically given up hope of ever finding him. Even in this situation, it was not possible to catch or pick him up. He was afraid and very cautious. All of us cats sensed that he was in some way reaching out for affection and help. Obviously fear held him back. There was nothing Donald could do as this bloody cat slipped off into the dark rainy night.

Incredibly! Amazingly! A little later in the night he climbed up the wisteria vine onto the loggia off Donald's study. It was clear that he knew that Donald was in there. It was still raining and Donald was at his desk when he heard something outside. He turned towards the glass door of the loggia and guess who was at the door? Yes, the cat, bloody and wet, staring at him with those incredible blue eyes. He made it very clear that he wanted in and now! Without hesitation, Donald opened the door and the poor thing bounced in with no trace of fear. Donald wrapped him in a towel and proceeded to clean off the blood and dry his rain-soaked body. He was totally calm and acted as if he had always been part of the family. That night he peacefully slept in the house. Donald said it reminded him of an old hymn called *Rescue the Perishing*. "Rescue the perishing, care for the dying, snatch them in pity . . . lift up the fallen . . . ".

You might say that at that moment he was actually adopted and became part of the family. This is one of those things that was meant to happen and was the opening revelation of a new story! Yes, there was no question that he was my offspring! There was a particular sense of our belonging to one another that was not shared with the other cats. He immediately bonded in a special way with Donald, who, just like he did for me, gave him a special name. It was to be Havana Banana, based on the visual similarity of his coat to a dessert Donald enjoyed in Miami. Of course, my name, Tiramisù is also a dessert, one of Italy's most famous! How sweet is that?

Havana Banana

Speaking of food, one of my favorite things is Chicken Curry, whether it be North Indian, South Indian, Thai Red, or Green Curry. All of them are delicious! There is something in my Thai/South Asian heritage that just launches me when hot chili curries are being served. Donald is really an expert chef in this field, and he observed that I would do just about anything to get some curry when he was serving it. So, he always made sure that I would get my portion. Our European cats did not seem to appreciate this delectable fare as much as I did. However, even they could never complain since only highly sought-after gourmet cat food, from organic fish to pâté de foie, was served on our plates. Donald saw to that!

One thing that I have not mentioned is that I really did not ever want Donald out of my sight. Whenever I saw him, I would come straight towards him making my little affection-ate meow and beg to be picked up and carried around like a sack of sugar. If he didn't get the picture, I would just give a claw-pull down on his jeans. Of course, that always got his atten-tion. I would have been more than content if he would've just packed me around for hours as if he had nothing else to do! If Donald sat down on the garden bench, I would immedi-ately jump up on his lap. Havana Banana often did the same and would try to wedge in as well. Snowshoes are known for being VERY attached to their "owners" (such a bad word!), but as far as we were concerned, there was never too much hugging and attention.

Even though I was such a "good" cat, I did a few things that really got Donald's ire. One was my habit of giving a good cat spray just when I felt like doing it which was usually in his presence. I figured that everything was part of my territory from the wheels of the parked car to the living room furniture, and I needed to mark it all. One of the worst things I did was climb up into the loggia off his study and insist—well, maybe demand—that Donald let me in. He was always busy in there preparing seminars which, I gathered, demanded his complete attention.

In the dark night of pouring rain through this loggia door I entered into a life of unconditional love, mercy, and compassion that healed my bloody wounds and embraced my hopeless lostness. —Havana Banana

Through this gate we, the cats, entered into a New Life!

But I wanted attention, too! After I finally persuaded him to let me in, I'd wander around his desk for a while and then scale the cabinets where he had placed some of his framed paintings. My explorations irritated Donald who was convinced that his paintings would come crashing down. He would scold me, *"Perchè fai questa confusione?"* And tell me to get down immediately. I would, but often I gave a "goodbye" squirt on the paintings before I exited the room. The delinquency of my behavior often left a permanent mark of my guilt.

I found out that in desperation, Donald finally went down to consult with Dr. Enrico. "Is it possible for a cat that has been castrated to continually want to spray on everything? I thought he would grow out of this." Dr. Enrico replied, "Well, it is not normal, but one never knows for sure. Is he a dominant type?" Donald answered, "Yes, he could be called a dominant type. He pretty much always gets his way and he is smarter than most of us!"

The trouble was that this bad behavior of mine got me banished from being inside much more than I would have liked, and when I was allowed inside, I was highly monitored. This, of course, became kind of a game for me—but I didn't dare cross the line!

Most of you would probably say, "*Basta!* Enough is enough! This cat is just too much; a real pest." Don't you worry, I have heard those words a time or two. The irritant of all irritants for Donald and Laura is when I jump on top of a rosemary, sage, thyme, or curry plant, do a wild war dance, and take a quick pee-pee. I do get a few cross words and a spanking on these occasions . . . but only if they can catch me. To be very honest with you, I don't know why or how they put up with me.

Some like a hot tub, but a hot stone sink with a view is even better!

Sometimes, when I am laying in the old stone sink in the courtyard, catching some sun with Baby Calico Skies and Salvatore, surrounded by all this beauty and peace, I ask, "Now how did I deserve all of this?" The fact is it has nothing to do with deserving! I have learned and experienced that it has everything to do with two words I hear frequently around this house. The first is *Agape*—unconditional love—which is not expressed because you are so nice and lovable; it's LOVE freely given because that is the best way. The second word is *Grace*—unmerited love and favor that can't be earned or bought—that which puts you in good standing and acceptance. Oh my goodness, I have certainly received a lot of this! This might sound a little heady, but even as a cat, it applies because I am one of God's creatures. Yes, all of us cats were deeply loved by Donald and Laura. No one was considered the favorite; we each had our own special personality.

From what I have told you so far, you can see that we lived way out in the countryside, isolated with wild boar, vineyards, and olive groves. But that did not stop the most interesting people from coming to our home, L'Uccellare. Donald and Laura frequently hosted guests: princesses and pop stars, classical musicians and comedians, and garden enthusiasts! The garden events were my favorites since we got to accompany the guests as they wandered around enjoying the beauty and smelling the roses. Donald often gave inspirational lectures followed by elegant sit-down dinners prepared by him and Laura. We cats were rarely allowed in the house for these events, but we watched all the goings-on through the ceiling-to-floor sliding glass doors of the *salone* where everyone was gathered.

And, if you can believe it, all of us "poor" orphan cats once got to hear Sir Paul (yes, *the* Paul McCartney), Donald and Laura's brother-in-law, singing and playing the piano. Not that we knew he was a celebrity or someone special. I tell you this because there is a story about Sir Paul and

the way Baby Calico Skies got her name. Sir Paul had written a song, *Calico Skies*, right around the time when Donald and Laura found her on that dirt road late at night. Donald loved that song, and seeing that Baby was a real calico cat, it just seemed perfect to name her Baby Calico Skies.

Laura and Baby Calico Skies

Okay, you are at your post, and I am at mine. We're on duty, so keep your eyes open!

Always at the end of these evening events, Donald would take a flashlight and walk the guests to their cars parked out in the field. Some of us cats would tag along beside Donald. The guests were so happy, and as we walked, they told Donald how much they enjoyed such a wonderful evening. All of this friendliness and kindness poured over on us cats as well, even though I have to admit that we really didn't do much to make the evening exceptional.

Life is full of beautiful surprises, and sadly, tragedies as well. As time passed we had to deal with illnesses and other unfortunate things. Most of us cats were rescued from very difficult situations and already had weaknesses. If it hadn't of been for the mercy and love of Donald and Laura, who knows where we would have ended up: we probably would have died a long time ago. I have mentioned that Santolina was one of my favorites and I always felt a special affection for her because she lost one of her eyes. But she, too, ended up having cat AIDS and her health went slowly downhill. There was no way to cure her and one day she, in her weakness, just passed on. It was very sad not having her around anymore with all of her hilarious antics.

Not too long after we lost Santolina, another stray cat appeared at the large gate of the courtyard and cautiously entered between the iron bars. He looked very wild. We had no idea where he came from, especially since we lived in such a remote area. Even though he was fully grown, he could have been tossed out by someone who had left the area. He meowed loudly and hissed when we approached him. But he was also very insistent: he was not going any place and had NO intention of leaving! Donald tried to scare him away, but it was not to be. His eyes were incredible with a very aggressive, almost attacking look, and his gaze penetrated right to your bones. However, we saw that he was desperate and behind those eyes there was a cry for help. Compassion won out and Donald and Laura said, "Let's just let him stay."

He seemed starved and when he was given food, he gobbled it down as if to say "Thank you, thank you." In just a few days after arrival, he was a transformed cat and ended up being a great friend to all of us. It shows what love and compassion can do. He still had those penetrating eyes, but they were no longer filled with fear or desperation: now he gazed

at you with deep affection. He would almost cry when he saw Donald and would jump up and down as if trying to control his emotions and the love—yes love—he felt for Donald. Jack the Cat was now totally part of our family.

Time was passing and everything seemed very settled and routine. We had been living these last years in this wide-open countryside, a delight for us all. There was great hunting in the tall grass; we never knew what we might run into. There were the lizards of all sizes and colors, field mice, and even a snake once in a while. Sometimes there were poisonous vipers which, of course, we would stay away from. For some reason snakes just don't like cats around and they decided to move on to some other territory. We would spend many hours just lounging around in the courtyard or exploring the orchards. It was great fun chasing each other up and down the huge fig trees in a game of "I bet you can't catch me." For us, this place was a paradise.

I bet you didn't know I could fly!

Then came a day when we overheard the words, "We're *all* moving to San Remo!" Of course, that meant nothing to us. It was more like a mystery in the air, something we sensed. Our Donald and Laura seemed very edgy which left us quite perplexed. I had no real clue as to what was happening, only that we began to see quite a few people coming in and out of the house and the gardens. The only thing I knew was that they certainly were not the typical friendly guests dropping by.

One day in early November, there was a big shuffle and almost everything was moved out of the house and loaded into big trucks. After all this commotion, the drivers said goodbye and departed up the road. Within a short time, Donald exited the house, kissed Laura goodbye, jumped into his car, and took off up the road. We didn't have a clue as to what was going on since Laura was left behind with us. We felt something wasn't quite right. This was not normal behavior. We could feel our daily serene routine and peace being turned upside down and coming to an end!

Donald returned a couple days later but no trucks! He rushed around and came out of the house with all the cat carriers and lined them up by the front door. You can imagine what went through our minds since the cat carriers meant something not pleasant was about to take place: shots or traumas or just making the trip up and down the steep hills to the vet. Donald and Laura began going around looking to locate all of us, calling our names one-by-one. We were a little stupefied by what was happening but we all declared "PRESENT!" which was no small feat considering that we often were on a "discovery outing" in the vineyards.

Here we were: Gioia, Baby Calico Skies, Salvatore, Benjamin, Havana Banana, Jack the Cat, and me. Before we knew what was happening, we were all picked up and caged and placed into the SUV with the suitcases leaving for who-knows-where. For how long? It was anyone's guess. It happened so fast and seemed so conclusive. The reality was, we were never to return to L'Uccellare in Chianti. This was our final goodbye!

It was a good four-hour trip starting on a late November afternoon. We were leaving Tuscany and all that we had ever known was left behind. It was what humans call "surreal". As we traveled, the sun was going down and before long we came into a dark downpour with rain pelting the windows, making the trip even more strange. Donald and Laura hardly said a word. Mile after mile we kept traveling when suddenly the storm clouds briefly opened onto a bright red and black sunset. Soon, the sunset turned into darkness. Now all we could see were headlights of cars and trucks rushing by in both directions. It was both strange and frightening. This went on for hours it seemed, and here we were all cuddled and stuffed into the carriers. Donald and Laura tried to encourage us saying, "Be patient. We'll soon be at our destination." Softly Laura said, "Don't worry, everything is going to be okay." Every so often they would whisper that we were now traveling on the Riviera coast of Liguria, which of course meant nothing to us, but just hearing their sweet voices gave us courage and lessened our anxiety.

After many hours, we finally arrived at the unknown destination, having put up with Benjamin and Baby Calico Skies crying the whole trip. The first impression from our cramped cages was that it was very dark. Nobody said a word, including me. We could tell that Donald and Laura were extremely nervous about our "landing." They were discussing how and when to release us so we would not scatter in every direction in complete darkness. Donald got out of the car and switched on some outdoor lighting which really did not illuminate much; it was pitch black in all directions. There were no other people around. Finally, we were taken out of the car to fearfully await our release into the unknown and unseen. It was scary to say the least! A strong, cold wind was blowing up from the sea and the surrounding palm fronds were dancing wildly. There was a very loud noise that we had never heard before; it sounded like it was coming right at us! Later, we learned that it was the roar of the waves pounding the shore.

San Remo—"Villa Gioiello"

Donald returned to the apartment again, turned on some house lights, and opened the door. That didn't help much; it was still very dark. Donald and Laura stood in silence with all of us—still caged—beside the car. Finally, Donald said, "Okay let's let them out! But first, a prayer, since they might go totally bonkers and flee the coop. I don't know; they may go crazy and with this darkness we can't even see where they go. All I can say is, 'God please help us!'"

They opened the latches and sure enough, we scattered in all directions in total panic; we had no idea where we were or where to go. It was a

horrible experience, just horrible!!! We went north, south, east, and west and only the voices of dear Donald and Laura calling out in calmness, and maybe in desperation, brought us to sanity. Soon, one by one, we all returned and gathered closely around their feet. They truly were our only shelter and comfort. "Don't be scared," they said. "We are here, and it will be alright. We won't leave you; no, we will not leave you."

Their kindness and gentleness and their love was so real. It made us feel at home even if we didn't know what happened to home. We were slowly coaxed and carried

48

into the small but cozy apartment. It was totally different and dis-
orienting compared to what we had left behind, but peace settled
in upon us. We *all* felt lost, but together, we felt found. The bed and
the bedroom were small, but before we knew it, all of us cats and
Laura—were on the bed for our first night's sleep on the Riviera
of Flowers. Yes, and even Donald eventually found a small slice of
bed upon which to rest his head. Despite everything, we slept cozily,
thankful to be snuggled together. What a comfort it was to be tightly
packed together!

Well, here we are, but I don't know where Donald is going to sleep.

It really is true that a house is not a home unless there is a shelter of love, serenity, and affection. In a short time, Donald transformed the terrace at Villa Nazareth into a place of beauty with many of the familiar pots of flowers from L'Uccellare and our favorite cushioned bench which just about accommodated all the cats. What more could we ask for? We were all getting on in years, quite content to laze in the sun and look out over the Mediterranean Sea. We didn't even mind sleeping outside in the sheltered veranda because our very familiar cat house had made the move with us.

While we lived at Villa Nazareth, Gioia, the oldest cat, finally began to slow down and needed frequent medical attention. This was sad for all of us to see. Gioia never did really embrace the other cats since she knew that she was the queen. Her attention was definitely focused on Laura. Gioia was very intelligent and, without any encouragement, learned Italian in her own way and even responded to questions in cat talk. One time in the wee hours of the night at an event at our home in Tuscany, a number of young Italian guys were joyfully chatting. Gioia was perched on the back of the couch where they were seated and Donald told the guys, "You'd be amazed to hear this, but Gioia understands and talks back when you speak to her."

"No, it is not possible!" they exclaimed.

"Listen, I will ask her a question, but not look directly at her, and she will answer me," Donald said.

He posed the question of whether or not she was enjoying this late evening get-together and of course she responded with a "meow, meow!" Everyone was quite taken back. This was not the only time this happened! Well, our dear Gioia was slowly passing away and no medicine could save her. She died in the night in the cat house while Donald petted and talked to her. He prayed over her and she was gone. We all felt the loss; we missed her so much. Donald buried her in the garden of the new house that we would be moving to after our apartment.

Finally, the day came for us to move to Villa Gioiello, the restored Art Nouveau villa in the city of San Remo, city of flowers and music. This was all explained just prior to our move. Even if it meant very little to us, it was nice to be informed about where we were going. No anxiety or trauma was part of this move, just a smooth transition to another beautiful place. It didn't take much adjustment. This new place was a huge villa with three flights of stairs and I have climbed them all! A solid high fence of steel surrounded the palm-filled garden and kept us cats safe.

Signor Donald and Signora Laura were very generous to give us their WHOLE bench.

Sometimes we need to remember that our lives are pretty "cushioned." Thank you dear God, Donald, and Laura.

Oh my goodness, a whole roast chicken! If I could just open this window . . .
—Benjamin

We would be living mostly in the garden which, in time, Donald transformed into a paradise. Here we had a completely new, customized cat house designed just for us by our architect friend, Micol. It was tucked under the veranda so it sheltered us from the rain and gave us a great view over the garden and the Mediterranean Sea. It was kind of a five-star cat villa where we could watch the boats of the fishermen and see the huge cruise ships pass by day and night. Years passed and

somehow, we felt like we were in retirement in these beautiful low-stress surroundings.

Of course, we still had our favorite bench and the lights of San Remo, combined with the moonlight over the sea and the city, made sitting on the garden bench with Donald and Laura at night . . . magical. Jack the Cat, Havana Banana, Salvatore, Baby Calico Skies, Benjamin, and me joined in a tight fit, all wrapped up in the beach towels

Jack the Cat

with a couple of us on their laps. I, of course, always asked Donald to hold me.

This may give you the impression that everything was always serene and cozy, but as in all of life, it was not to be. Baby Calico Skies grew sick and weak after we moved. Despite the antibiotics, she just withered away and one day she disappeared, never to be seen again. It was a very sad moment for all of us. Now, there were only five of us cats.

Then one day a horrible incident occurred. We had a huge problem with giant seagulls that were very aggressive and were even known to have attacked the people of San Remo on the head. They would fly in and do everything to steal our food which, of course, was often fish. On this particular day, one swooped down on us as we were eating. I tried to defend us, but the seagull was determined and with his large beak went straight for my eye. He pulled out one of my eyeballs! It just hung there still attached on a "string" on my face!!! Donald, rushing to meet prospective custodians who were coming in by train from Milano, just happened to pass by me and saw what had happened. Praise God he passed exactly in that moment or who knows when it would have been seen. He went into a state of panic and called for Laura to come as quickly as possible. Seeing this horrible thing, they got me into the cat carrier, not wasting one minute, and Laura rushed me to the nearest vet.

Meanwhile, Donald was trying to monitor my situation via cellphone with Laura, and at the same time meet this couple and interview them for a possible work contract. You can imagine how *that* interview went with Donald knowing that my eye was hanging out of its socket while remaining calm enough to politely talk to the couple as if all was totally normal. Of course, with all the hysteria, no contract even came close to being signed; it was kind of a disaster!!

While all that was taking place I found myself in Animal Emergency with this vet who, thankfully, was considered the best in town. He took my dangling eyeball and carefully put it back in place. All of this took time, but by God's wonderful grace—and the precise hand of the vet—my eye was saved. I healed quickly, my eyesight still as sharp as ever. As we say, "Never a dull day!"

🐾 🐾 🐾

Always, and I mean *always* without fail, I am at the garden gate to greet my parents, Donald and Laura, when they return home day or night. I get a loving "ciao" and a pet and do one of my flip-flops. I love them soooooo much that I roll over with joy when I see them. To you, it may seem exaggerated, but it gives me a special feeling. I am so happy to see them.

We have learned that there are two categories of people regarding cats. One grouping usually dislikes them and makes that known to all. Then there are those that just LOVE cats. As soon as someone rings in at the villa, we can sense from a distance whether they are the friendly or the unfriendly type. If unfriendly, we quickly disappear and hide until they leave the property. But if someone friendly is at the gate, even if it's a stranger, we meet them with a warm greeting and express our happiness for their visit. It's like we can smell friendliness drifting in the air.

Laura with Benjamin

Or, a strange odor, rather unpleasant, if the visitor is someone who might say, "I just don't like or relate to cats. Dogs, yes. Cats, no. You can't make them do what you want. Have you ever heard of taking cats to a training or obedience school?" That is why we stayed out of sight when certain people came by the villa. I must say they are the minority.

Micol, the architect responsible for the restoration of Villa Gioiello (she also designed our luxurious cat house) is a very close friend of Laura and Donald and also a lover of cats. She knows our names and always greets us with delight. We reciprocate with a nice *ciao meow* and an affectionate flip-over and proceed to accompany her to the house. We can even tell she's arriving by the sound of her Vespa or her steps coming up the stairs to the garden.

Affection and love are like catnip, they draw you close, but indifference and arrogance are repelling. People love the fact that we are welcoming with, "*Ciao, benvenuto!*" and friendly at their first step through the gate. We have learned that to love and to be loved, mixed with kindness, is not a small thing.

I must gratefully admit that despite all of my bad habits and behavior, I am loved, and yes, adored. An orphan, tossed in a ditch, perhaps thrown out of a car, I had really no hope to be saved. Yet, Donald and Laura chose me, wanted me, adopted me, and I became their baby cat. Yes, they actually chose me when they could have said "no." This is love and compassion. Did they get a good deal? I think so. I sure did.

Signor Donald has helped me put into words what I want to say: The life of so many of us cats (and humans) is one of desperation, starvation, and hopelessness. For many, life is very cheap. If you are in the way, you are abandoned or worse. No remorse. But Love and Grace walk another road and intersect with Mercy, Compassion, and Kindness. They reach out to heal, to feed, and to quench that thirst, whatever it may be: physical, emotional, or spiritual. Together they embrace and shelter you in love and affection. You belong. You get a special name. Yes, grace and love are a real "Tiramisù."

🐾 🐾 🐾

THE END

🐾 🐾 🐾

*"Your unfailing love , O Lord, is as vast as the heavens:
your faithfulness reaches beyond the clouds."*

*"You care for people and animals alike, O Lord.
How precious is your unfailing love, O God!"*

"All humanity finds shelter in the shadow of your wings."

Psalm 36: 5,6b,7 Holy Bible—New Living Translation

ACKNOWLEDGMENTS

Acknowledgments from Tiramisu, the cat:

to Giovanna Nannoni, because she . . .

- 🐾 rescued me from death as a tiny abandoned kitten, and got me a home.
- 🐾 showed compassion and mercy.
- 🐾 believed in love and goodness, and that I was worth saving.

to Micol Maiga, because we loved seeing her; why? . . .

- 🐾 her warm personal kindness.
- 🐾 she talked to me, and called me by name.
- 🐾 her love got us a five-star cat house.

to Lisa Fugard, because she helped my Donald, . . .

- 🐾 get through the tough moments of putting together my story.
- 🐾 with her friendly encouragement and gentleness to relax and believe that a book would finally happen.

THE AUTHORS

TIRAMISÙ, born in 1997 in the Reggello area near Florence, Italy, died on August 19, 2015, in San Remo, Italy, living 18 incredible years. Having been abandoned and orphaned, he nearly died in 1997 of trauma from Immune Deficiency (cat AIDS). Prayer and love brought healing and hope for a kitten destined to hopelessness. His friend, Jack the Cat died two weeks later, on September 2, 2015.

🐾 🐾 🐾

DONALD JAMES MALCOLM was raised on a ranch in Paradise Valley, Montana near Yellowstone National Park. He often rode his horse to the one-room school house, or forded the Yellowstone River to catch a bus. For his college studies he went to So. California and received his BA degree at Biola University, and some years later did a Master's Degree in Biblical Studies.

His life calling was a mission to see transformed lives among the needy and the hurting whether it was U.S. colleges, Mexican villages, remote areas in Malawi, the 38 years living in Italy, and the challenges of Afghanistan where he designed and created "The Garden of Peace and Hope" in Kabul dedicated to young artists and musicians. With his wife, Laura, they also continue a partnering mission of humanitarian help to the poor and the abused of India.

It is true that, it is more blessed to give than to receive.

*"Give justice to the poor and the orphan; uphold the rights of the oppressed
and the destitute. Rescue the poor and helpless; deliver them from the grasp
of evil people. They have neither knowledge nor understanding,
they walk about in darkness;..."*
—*Psalm 82:3-5*

🐾 🐾 🐾

"Amazing grace how sweet the sound that saved a wretch like me.
I once was lost, but now am found. Was blind but now I see.
Thru many dangers, toils and snares I have already come;
'Tis grace hath brought me safe thus far, And grace will lead me home."
—"Amazing Grace" John Newton, 1725-1807